Ronan and Macy

By Eliza Whoriskey O'Neill

Illustrations by Suzanna Marshall

Publisher: Inspiring Publishers,
P.O. Box 159, Calwell, ACT Australia 2905
Email: publishaspg@gmail.com
http://www.inspiringpublishers.com

 A catalogue record for this book is available from the National Library of Australia

National Library of Australia The Prepublication Data Service

Author: Eliza Whoriskey O'Neill
Title: Ronan and Macy
Genre: Fiction
ISBN: 978-0-6451228-0-0

For Clara and Tate

Ronan awoke as he heard Ann enter the kitchen. As the late fall sun rose, she quickly dished him his breakfast and then gazed out the window towards the brightening horizon. Before he could wonder why things were getting started so early, she said, "Now Ronan, we

must be on our best behavior this morning. A nice lady from New York City is coming up to look at your sister, Macy. We want her to find a good home, don't we?"

It was more of a statement than a question, but either way, Ronan wasn't so sure. He knew Ann had been struggling for months to find a suitable home for Macy, the smallest pup born seven months ago in Tilda's last litter, weighing only seven ounces. Still tiny by the breed standard at just 20 pounds, Ann knew Macy was unlikely to turn into the prize-winning show dog so many of her sisters and brothers had. Hard as it was to part with the pup's sweet, shy, and loving nature, Ann had to now find Macy a good home, so she could keep her focus on the responsibilities at the farm - the chickens and their eggs, the fruits and vegetables grown on the grounds; and the wildly popular muffins she and her daughter Mel made to sell at the weekly Saturday markets in town.

"We can't keep another doggie, I'm afraid," Ann had told Ronan. "You're enough dog for us," she said as she patted him under his neck, making his tail thump on the floor like a drum.

Indeed, he was. At nearly 160 pounds, Ronan took up quite a large amount of space in their small country house and seemed to eat more than Ann and Mel combined on most days. His heart was as big as his appetite though, and Ronan was the most loving and sensitive dog Ann had ever known.

After his morning nap, Ronan rose to stretch, feeling Macy release herself from his side. They had snuggled this way ever since Tilda weaned her. Macy loved her big brother more than anything, and this morning she felt especially protected by the warmth of his thick and soft double coat. Ronan had been one of six pups born in Tilda's first litter five years ago. With all the latest litter pups besides Macy sold to show dog owners, it was time for Tilda to retire and rest on the farm. Ronan would soon follow, but for now he knew he had a job to do. If his favorite little sister had to go to a new home, he would make sure it was a good one.

· · ·

Ronan had been doing quite a bit of work behind the scenes over the past few weeks to ensure that a range of unsuitable potential paw-rents had <u>no</u> chance of adopting Macy. On Monday, Don Scratch, a man who already had twelve cats, three parrots, two hamsters and a lizard came by to try to make her his next acquisition.

When Ronan heard Don telling Ann about his house full of cat litter and his desire for a dog who could, "entertain" his feline friends, Ronan approached Don with his most regal stance and leapt up with a bark that shook the walls. Frightened, Don quickly thanked Ann and scurried out the door. Ronan and Macy exchanged a furry high five as he sped away down the road.

Then came Wednesday, when they were visited by Ms. Putzey and her nine-year-old daughter, Laney. Ms. Putzey authoritatively strode into the house, bringing with her a powerful aroma of hairspray, perfume and chewing gum that almost knocked Ann, Macy and Ronan on their sides. Laney followed her mother inside with a pout, phone in hand, and filmed the visit from start to finish for her YouTube channel, *AbsoLaney Awesome*. Ms. Putzey intently stroked Macy's fur, closely examining it. "Oh, this will do quite nicely!" she shrieked, explaining that her online business, Fur-fection, sold authentic canine fur accessories, including keychains, makeup brushes, good luck charms and stuffed animals. A record year in sales was attributed, of course, to marketing on *AbsoLaney Awesome*.

Ronan could not fathom the idea of his sister's fur being sheared to sell a $9 stuffed toy and tried to control his shock and horror. He quickly gave Macy the secret nudge that only he and she knew what to do with. In rapid succession, Ronan lifted a leg as Macy squatted, and all of a sudden, both of Laney's perfect pink patent leather shoes were graced with a warm, wet puddle. She yelled out with a shrill scream, "Eeeeewwww! These are the most disgusting dogs in the world! I'm leaving ... right ... this ... minute!" And without even a chance for Laney's mother to adjust her bouffant, the two scrambled out the door, into the car and back to wherever it was they had come from.

"All of this work sending people away is fun, but it sure is exhausting," Macy said to Ronan as they settled down for their afternoon snooze.

"Yes," Ronan agreed, "but it's worth it for you." He continued calmly, "We will find you a good home, Macy, I promise."

Macy thought for a minute before replying, "Ronan, you will always be my brother, but I know Ann and Mel have their hands full here, and I could probably be a good companion to someone who needs me." She continued, "If I knew I could see you every once in a while and have fun with an owner who was kind and caring, well then, I might not be so sad to leave."

Ronan was surprised to hear this, but also proud that his sister had reached the milestone when every pup knows they are ready to make another family complete. He was filled with sadness nonetheless and drifted off to sleep thinking of all of the siblings he had seen leave home before her. Many were prize-winning show dogs, and their days at the farm had been brief. But Macy had been with him so much longer, and their bond was stronger than any of the others. Whimpering, he tried not to think about the idea of losing her forever, the first thought that had ever been truly unbearable to him.

. . .

The next morning, Ronan and Macy stayed snug and warm by the fireplace for a bit longer than usual. When Macy started to prop herself up from the curve of Ronan's belly and had a look outside, she couldn't believe what she saw. The ground was covered with a magical layer of white, quickly accumulating as flakes fell fast from the sky. Macy's first snowfall did not disappoint. She nudged Ronan and moved closer to the doorway, signaling for him to see the beauty for himself. After a stretch and survey of the landscape, Ronan let out his customary low howl by the doorway, signaling to whoever was alert in the adult world to let them out for a nice long play.

After almost an hour outside, a small SUV came slowly and carefully up the slippery drive. 'Oh no ... not again,' thought Ronan as he studied the stranger getting out of the car - a middle aged woman with weather-proof boots and a parka draping her petite frame. Sensibly dressed, at least, Ronan thought as he approached the gate and prepared to let out one of his intimidating barks to deter the visitor. But something stopped him. The woman, looking calmly at him and Macy, had a kind face and a stance that seemed to reflect respect and patience. Ronan backed away and deciding to give her the benefit of the doubt at least for a moment, lay down on the snowy grass, with Macy joining him at his side.

"Well, hello there," the woman said. "I'm Marjorie Simms, from the big City. You must be Ronan, and you must be little Macy."

Marjorie bent down to give each dog a generous pat around the neck, reaching under the collar, their favorite sweet spot. Macy wagged her tail excitedly, feeling the warmth of this stranger, and rolled over, hoping for a belly rub. Marjorie didn't hesitate, affectionately rubbing her tummy with both bare hands. Ann then appeared at the door, looking exasperated from her work in the kitchen. She was prepared to give Marjorie a total of ninety seconds before sending her away like all the others who had come before.

"Good morning. Ann is it?" said Marjorie. "I decided to leave earlier from New York so I could get here in time to avoid ice on the roads. I seem to have just made it."

"Yes, well you sure did," replied Ann, sensing the sincerity in Marjorie's tone, and softening her own just a bit. "So, you came all the way from New York City, then? We have more and more city folks buying weekend homes here lately. I've only been there twice myself, both times to see one of our dogs compete in the Westminster Dog Show."

"Oh yes, that is a favorite of mine!" exclaimed Marjorie with sincere enthusiasm.

Ann offered Marjorie a cup of coffee and one of Mel's homemade blueberry muffins. "My, these are delicious!" said Marjorie. "My late husband just adored homemade blueberry muffins, and so do my children. I must get the recipe from you."

"We sell these muffins every weekend at the Farmer's Market in the Village Square, and I'm happy to say that on a typical Saturday morning we usually sell out within forty-five minutes," Ann said.

"Wow, that is quite something." said Marjorie. "You should think about bringing them to New York."

Ann gave it a second's thought before replying, "Yes, well that seems like an awful lot of trouble. But we're grateful for their popularity. It helps us stay afloat here on the farm, especially with all of the rising costs these days."

"I'm sure it does," said Marjorie.

She continued, "I've lived in New York for nearly thirty years, ever since my husband and I married." She continued, "I was raised as a country girl myself, but after all these years I've come to love it. As a child, I had a Bernese Mountain Dog named Luke, who I adored.

I retired last June, and my husband, Bill, passed away a few weeks later. With our three children all grown, I thought it might be a good time to have a companion again."

"I see," said Ann. "So, you live in an apartment? ..."

Marjorie could tell where Ann's mind was going and eagerly jumped back in, "Yes, it's a good size and right by the park. In fact, I walk in Central Park twice every day, and love meeting the other dogs and owners there. Manhattan really is a very dog-friendly city. When I saw your ad that mentioned Macy was a smaller size for a Bernese, I thought she could be a perfect fit for me."

"Well yes, I suppose that does sound like it could be alright for her," said Ann. "But I'm not sure. What do you think, Ronan?"

Ronan crossed his paws, a unique Berner trait that always made it seem to Ann as if he were deep in thought. He kept his gaze on Marjorie.

Ann continued, "And what about you, Ms. Macy, what do you think?"

Macy wagged her tail and bumped up against Marjorie's side, hinting for another under-the-collar rub.

"They are very close, you see," said Ann. "I've had more than 20 of these dogs over my lifetime, and I've never seen a bond quite like these two."

"That is a very special thing," replied Marjorie, patting Macy, who delightedly kept wagging her tail as she rolled over again.

"Well then, Ronan, perhaps we could come back and visit you sometime, to make sure you don't forget your sister?" Marjorie said.

'How could I EVER forget her?' Ronan thought, as a tear welled up in his eye.

"I'm sure they would like that," said Ann. Not wanting to dwell in the emotion of the moment and seeing for herself how happy Macy seemed to be with Marjorie, she said, "I guess it's settled then. I'll get her bed, chew toys and some food to start you off."

Ronan got up and stood next to Macy, nudging her snout with his usual Berner bump, as he held back tears in his sad, dark eyes. Macy nudged Ronan back and together, the two of them went out front for one last run in the snow.

"I am so grateful to you for giving me the opportunity to have Macy," said Marjorie. "She is a sweet, special pup, and I promise I will take the very best care of her, always."

And with that, Marjorie scooped up little Macy and secured her safely in the back of the car. "Goodbye," said Marjorie, "and thank you."

"Goodbye," said Ann.

Ronan lay down, crossing his paws in resignation and burying his head in the snow as if he were trying to duck under the covers to avoid the reality of what was happening.

He spent the rest of the day under the kitchen table, barely eating or sleeping, just thinking of what he was going to do without his baby sister, and best friend.

Just before bedtime, when Ann could sense Ronan was in a state of despair, she gave him a pat on his belly and softly said, "Now Ronan, I was afraid this would happen. You have been through this many times before, and this time is no different. Macy has found a good, loving home, with someone who will be able to care for her and give her everything she needs. You will be fine. I know you will," she said.

But as she tried herself to fall asleep that night, Ann wasn't at all sure that what she had said was the truth.

. . .

Two weeks later, after days of baking non-stop in preparation for the last Saturday market of the season, Ann and Mel were hoping for a day of record muffin sales. Ronan, still downcast and missing Macy, half-interestedly looked out the front doorway and saw the two women packing loads of muffins into the truck. Barely touching his breakfast, he decided to go back to sleep. After all, there was no one to play with anymore, no one to teach the ropes to, or to protect, or to cuddle with.

Just before heading out, Ann looked back and said, "Ronan, why don't you come along with us today?" It had been months since Ronan went to the Saturday markets. He used to enjoy a lot of pats and attention from admiring townspeople and weekend city slickers. He would even occasionally score a good belly rub or two and some treats. But today, he just didn't feel like it. He missed his sister, and he was sad. He wanted to be alone.

But Ann pressed. "Come on now," she said.

Ronan sluggishly approached the truck, and Mel helped him into the back.

When they arrived at the village square, Ann and Mel could see that it would be a record day, with folks stocking up on all of their favorite goodies before the long winter set in. It seemed that with each week, there were more and more folks coming from the city; those who had bought country homes here or who were just visiting for the weekend. Although it was good for business, more city folks meant the costs of living in what was once a quiet and sleepy rural village were creeping up.

They set up their tent and began selling as soon as the market opened. A line of people quickly stretched down the length of the square and around the bend, everyone was there for the best blueberry muffins on the east coast, according to loyal patrons.

Ronan, for his part, stayed under the tent on all fours and with his head on the ground. He wasn't in the mood for pats, or even belly rubs. He was just there because Ann and Mel had made him come.

After nearly three hours and more than 2,000 muffins sold, they were down to their last few boxes of four. Although the line still stretched long, Mel graciously told the remaining hopeful buyers that they were nearly all sold out, and only the next ten customers in line would be served.

The folks who had been waiting so long were disappointed. Gradually they accepted they would have to wait until spring to taste the delicacies again, and they moved out of the line.

Then Ann recognized the voice of a woman who, thrilled with her luck, had received one of the last boxes of muffins for sale. "Oh, thank goodness," the woman exclaimed. Just as Ann raised her head from the table to see who it was, she heard the clang of a dog tag against a leash, and saw the faint brush of a brown, white and black coated small dog wag its tail as it started to explore.

"Could it be?" she said to herself.

"Hello, Ann. Hello, Mel. And Hello, Ronan!" Marjorie greeted them cheerfully as she approached the muffin table, with Macy, now just a bit bigger and eagerly wagging her tail at her side. "I'm thrilled that I got one of the last boxes. My children are visiting next week for Thanksgiving, and I promised them I would get a box or two for breakfast here at our new place."

"Your new place?" asked Ann.

"Yes," Marjorie replied. "I just fell in love with it here when I came to pick up Macy. I decided it would be the perfect place for a country home where my children could come visit and where Macy and Ronan could run and play together. I hope that would be okay with you, if Ronan came for a puppy playdate sometime?"

Ronan, upon seeing Macy, leapt up as fast as he could. Running to his sister, and forgetting he was on a long leash tied to the table leg, he knocked the entire table over, scattering the remaining baked goods all over the cold ground.

Ronan nudged Macy's side and snout, rolling over with her and playing in the now falling snow. Their tails fiercely wagging, it was a sight to see, a joyful reunion that had both pups pouncing with pleasure.

"Why yes," said Ann, a wide smile spreading across her face. "I think that would be just perfect."

About the Author

Eliza O'Neill was born and raised in suburban Westchester County, New York.

She worked for nearly two decades in the healthcare sector before relocating to Sydney in 2019 with her husband, Colin and two daughters, Tate and Clara. They are looking forward to being reunited with their dog Ronan, in Australia in 2021.

CPSIA information can be obtained
at www.ICGtesting.com
Printed in the USA
LVHW070833100921
697439LV00010B/239